BUILDING CHRISTIAN CHARACTER

GILLY GREENWEED'S
GIFT FOR
GRANNY

A BOOK ABOUT
SHOWING LOVE

Michael P. Waite
Illustrated by Barbara Wdowski DeRosa

Chariot Books™
David C. Cook Publishing Co.

To the model child, Andrea, and to her beaming
parents, Warren and Robin, whose friendship is an
irreplaceable gift. MPW

Thanks be to Mike, Gary, Jill, and Tony for all the
laughs, encouragement, patience, help, and hard
work. BWD

Chariot Books™ is an imprint of David C. Cook Publishing Co.
David C. Cook Publishing Co., Elgin, Illinois 60120
David C. Cook Publishing Co., Weston, Ontario
Nova Distribution Ltd., Newton Abbot, England
GILLY GREENWEED'S GIFT FOR GRANNY
© 1992 by Michael P. Waite for text and illustrations

Designed by Studio North
First Printing, 1992
Printed in the United States of America
96 95 94 93   5 4 3 2
Library of Congress Cataloging-in-Publication Data
Waite, Michael P., 1960-
    Gilly Greenweed's Gift for Granny / Michael P. Waite; illustrated by Barbara Wdowski DeRosa.
    p. cm. — (Building Christian character)
    Summary: Gilly worries about not having a present for Granny's birthday, until she discovers that the best present is her love.
    ISBN 0-7814-0035-X
    [1. Birthdays—Fiction. 2. Gifts—Fiction. 3. Grandmothers—Fiction. 4. Stories in rhyme.]
I. DeRosa, Barbara, ill. II. Title. III. Series: Waite, Michael P., 1960- Building Christian character.
PZ83.W136G1 1992   91-37443
[E]—dc20   CIP   AC

Deep in the reeds and the bogwater weeds
That grow in the shallows of Pollywog Pond,
A small cottage rests
'Neath the wild watercress—
The coziest hut on the bog and beyond!

4

Snug in this cranny lives dear little Granny,
Who just had a birthday a short while ago.
This birthday is why
Gilly Greenweed stopped by
To stay with her Granny a few days or so.

Oh my, they had fun! They swam in the sun.
They went for a stroll by the shore.

They chatted with frogs
And with turtles on logs,
And picked purple plants by the score!

They stayed up all night by the soft firelight
Working on puzzles and sipping on tea.
They chattered and giggled,
They snuggled and wiggled,
Till Gilly dozed off on her grandmother's knee.

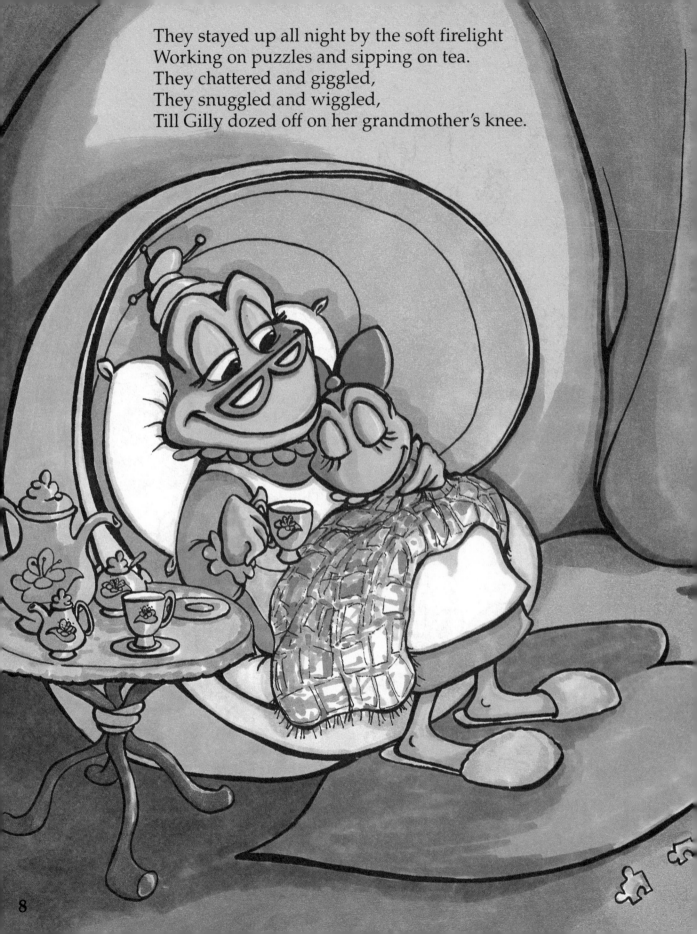

Early next morning, with Granny still snoring,
Gilly got breakfast set out on a tray.

"Oh my! What is this?"
Granny said with a kiss,
"What a marvelous present to start off my day!"

Just then came a rap, and a rat-a-tat-tap,
And in through the doorway came Cousin McMoe.
That dapper young fella
Set down his umbrella
And out of his coat took a box with a bow.

"I stopped by, you know, just to say cheerio!"
He stated while tipping his hat,
"And to give you this present,
You'll find it quite pleasant.
Happy Birthday! Best Wishes! All that!

13

"Now I must hurry off!" he exclaimed with a cough,
"I'm playing some polo today!
Tallyho! Off I go!"
Parted Cousin McMoe
And he gallantly galloped away.

The gift was a necklace of seashells with speckles,
Pretty as stars in the sky!
But Gilly felt awful
For not being thoughtful—
"I've no gift for Granny!" she sighed.

15

At noontime they napped
And they lunched and relaxed
Out in the cool of the weeds.

And while Granny dozed
With both her eyes closed,
Gilly wove presents from reeds!

Just as she finished her basket for Granny,
A buzzing sound shattered the air.
Out of the sky
Came a big dragonfly
And landed not far from her chair!

Down from the wing of that big buggish thing
Descended Aunt Olga and old Uncle Gip.
By their bright rosy clothes
Little Gilly supposed
That they'd come from some tropical trip!

"Howdy-doo!" shouted Olga.
"We came like we told ya!
We've just been to Billabong Bay,
Where we got ya this gifty—
It's real neat-o nifty!
We're sure awful sad we can't stay!"

Then old Uncle Gip, with the speed of a whip,
Was snapping off photos like mad!
They waved and they cried,
"Send a postcard! Good-bye!"
And they buzzed away looking quite sad.

Poor Gilly's eyes opened wide with surprise,
As out of the box came a pot,
And some teacups so tiny,
So silvery-shiny—
"What good is my basket?" she thought.

All through the night, Gilly worked in a fright,
Till her poor little back had grown stiff;
"I have failed!" Gilly wailed.
"Though I've pasted and nailed,
I can't make a good enough gift!

"But I have to keep trying!"
She muttered while crying,
"Or Granny will think I don't care.
Oh what can I give her
To prove that I love her?"
She dropped to her bed in despair.

Long before dawn, Granny woke with a yawn,
And there at the foot of her bed
Sat a huge wooden box,
As heavy as rocks,
With a little note written in red.

The note said, "To Granny, This gift is from Gilly
I know that it's not very good.
But I want you to know,
That I do love you so,
And I'd give you the world if I could!"

"What ever could be in this box?" wondered Granny,
She lifted and prodded and pried. . . .

And what a surprise!
Just imagine her eyes
When she found Gilly sleeping inside!

"Oh Granny!" said Gilly, feeling quite silly,
"I've nothing to give you, you see.
I worked all night through,
But the best I could do
Was to give you a box full of me."

"What a marvelous, glorious, beautiful present!"
Cried Granny while hugging her girl,

"I'd rather have you
And the sweet things you do
Than all of the gifts in the world!"

29

Now if you should happen past Pollywog Pond
And secretly peek from above,
You'll still find our Gilly
Showing that, really,
The very best present is love!